THE GOLDEN HEART OF WINTER

WRITTEN BY
MARILYN SINGER

ILLUSTRATED BY
ROBERT RAYEVSKY

MORROW JUNIOR BOOKS
NEW YORK

Thanks to Steve Aronson and
Joe Morton for their help.
—M.S.

Ink, watercolors, and acrylic were used for the full-color art.
The text type is 14 point Bernhard Modern.

Text copyright © 1991 by Marilyn Singer
Illustrations copyright © 1991 by Robert Rayevsky
Inquiries should be addressed to
William Morrow and Company, Inc.,
1350 Avenue of the Americas, New York, NY 10019.
Printed in Hong Kong at South China Printing Company (1988) Ltd.

1 2 3 4 5 6 7 8 9 10

Library of Congress Cataloging-in-Publication Data
Singer, Marilyn.
The Golden Heart of Winter / Marilyn Singer ; illustrated by
Robert Rayevsky.
p.   cm.
Summary: To determine who will become master of their father's
smithy, three brothers vie for the Golden Heart that makes the
seasons turn.
ISBN 0-688-07717-X. — ISBN 0-688-07718-8 (lib. bdg.)
[1. Fairy tales.]   I. Rayevsky, Robert, ill.   II. Title.
PZ8.S3576Go 1991
[E]—dc20   90-35346 CIP AC

To Meredith Charpentier
for her patience and perseverance
—M.S.

To Ellen Friedman
—R.R.

When the leaves were crisping and the grass glowed in its final burst of green, a blacksmith felt the autumn in his sinews, laid down his hammer on his anvil, and called to his three sons.

"No one can make a sword that sings like I can," the eldest was boasting.

"My knives are so fine, they fly from their masters' hands without being thrown," the second son bragged, waving a dagger before him.

"Enough!" bellowed their father. "Be quiet and listen to me." He looked around the forge. "Where is Half?"

"Here, Father," his youngest son said from the corner where he'd been watching a mouse. Half, so named by his brothers, did not make knives or swords. No one would let him near the forge, for they all thought him a fool. Instead, he fetched wood for the furnace and cleaned out the ashes. And he was very good at soothing the horses that had to be shod.

The blacksmith looked at his sons and shook his head sadly. "I am tired," he said. "I am growing old. Soon I will lay down my hammer for the last time. I would have all three of you run this smithy, but I see that it cannot be. Therefore, one of you alone must take my place."

"Then that one shall be me," said the eldest son.

"No, no. It shall be me," insisted the second son.

Half said nothing at all.

The blacksmith raised his hand. "Listen well and learn how I shall choose my heir. Go forth, each of you, and bring back something of value. Whatever is worth the most will mark the master of this forge."

The two eldest sons looked at each other. Then they turned to Half, who was studying a beetle scuttling across the floor.

"This half-wit as well is to go on such a quest?" The eldest laughed.

"Yes, he will go. He, too, is my son."

"But, Father . . ." the second son began.

"No more words. There will be time enough for words when you return."

The next day, the eldest brother, hoping to get a head start, slipped out of the house at dawn. He strode swiftly along until he came to a crossroads, at the center of which was a great rock that glittered like a starry night. He chose the right-hand path, and it led him straight into a forest that was said to be magical. The eldest brother had always avoided this place. But as it was a shortcut to the town beyond and he was in a hurry, he decided to go on.

He walked quickly, paying little attention to the strange blossoms and to the skittering creatures that crossed his path. He was thinking, What thing of great value can I bring my father? when a harsh croak made him stumble. "What was that?" he shouted, his eyes darting wildly until they lit upon a blighted oak tree. In the trunk was a hollow like an oval window, and inside the hollow sat a thin and ragged raven, regarding him with sorrowful eyes.

"*Cr-ruck!*" she cried again, craning her neck toward him, holding the rest of her body stiff as if it were frozen in place.

"Quiet, you ugly bird," said the eldest brother. He gave a little shake and hurried on his way, but he could not tell one tree from another nor one glade from the next, and soon he was quite lost.

Meanwhile, the second brother, who'd started out close behind, was standing at the crossroads where the shining boulder lay. He chose the left-hand path. But it, too, led to the very same wood. He charged down a twisting trail, wondering what valuable thing he could bring his father. Suddenly, an anguished cry made him jump.

"Who's there?" he yelled, backing against a bush. Then he saw the raven in the oak tree. The bird gazed at him with pleading eyes and cawed once more. "Shut up, foul creature," the second brother said, and hurled a stone that glanced off the bird's wing. But this time the raven made no sound. The second brother went on his way, and in a little while he, too, was lost in the forest.

Now Half had not been in such a hurry as his brothers. There was the cat to be fed, the dog to be scratched, the latest uneasy horse to be comforted before he could depart. And along the way there were so many things to see and to collect—pretty stones and delicate twigs, blue and gray feathers, seed pods and leaves. It was nearly midafternoon when Half came to the magical forest.

Half knew this forest very well, for he spent much of his time here when he could leave his tasks. It was as friendly to him as his hearth, perhaps friendlier. He walked slowly through the wood, pausing here to gaze at the subtle purple of a flower, there to greet a bounding deer. He was thinking of what it would be like to live in the forest all year long when he heard a voice say, "Help me."

He looked to his right, but saw no one.

"Help me," said the voice again.

Half looked to his left, but there was nothing save a stand of pines.

"Help me," spoke the voice a third time. "Or I shall forever be imprisoned in this tree."

This time Half looked straight ahead and saw the miserable raven in the hollow of the oak.

"Are you speaking to me?" he asked.

"Yes. In plain speech I beg you to free me from this tree. Alone I cannot leave."

"What can I do to help you?"

"Lift me out, but be careful that my wings do not brush the walls of this hollow."

Half did as he was told.

As soon as the raven was free, she twitched from beak to tail, gave a great shudder and a sigh, unfolded her wings, and flew high up above the trees.

Half watched her with wide eyes.

In another moment, she returned and perched on a low branch before him. "Thank you," she said. "Thank you very much indeed. You have done a great kindness."

Half smiled. "You're very welcome. But tell me, why couldn't you leave the tree by yourself?"

"Ah, that is quite a story."

"Good," said Half. "I love stories."

"Then I'll gladly tell it to you." When Half had seated himself on the ground, the raven began. "Long ago, the twins Life and Death had to decide who would rule the world. Life wished that nothing would die. Death wanted nothing to live. Finally, they made a pact. There would always be Death amidst Life. There would always be Life amidst Death. And each would have its season." The raven paused.

Half sat quietly, mouth open, waiting for her to continue.

"But Life did not trust Death, and so, to make certain that spring would always come again, Life decided to bury beneath the ground a golden heart that would beat forever, stirring the roots and seeds, causing the sap to flow at its appointed time. Death agreed to this condition, but added another: If the Golden Heart of Winter were ever removed from its place, there would no longer be spring. No buds would swell or petals unfurl. No nestlings would chirp or colts run in the fields. Death alone would reign forever. To this Life agreed.

"For a long time, both were satisfied with this pact. But eventually Death grew tired of this shared reign. Now Death means to have the Golden Heart and rule alone."

Half felt a shiver begin at his toes and chase up his spine. "But I still don't understand. What has this to do with why you couldn't leave that tree?"

"Death put me there. I am the Golden Heart's guardian. I know where the heart lies. Death tried to force me to reveal that secret. But I would not."

"And is the heart still safe?"

"The heart still beats beneath the ground. You, young man, may hear it if you pass close to where it lies."

Half's eyes grew bright with excitement. "Would you take me there? I'd like to hear a heart beat deep within the earth."

The raven regarded him solemnly. "That I cannot do. But because you have a kind heart I will give you a riddle, and if you solve it you may perhaps find the place yourself."

Into Half's ear she whispered,

Up and down
Left and right
They criss and cross
Both day and night.
Under the sky
Under the ground
Under the starstone
It is found.

"Hmmm. That is a tricky riddle," said Half.
"I will have to think about it."
"I will leave you to do just that," said the raven.
And away she flew to report Death's treachery to Life.

Half sat on the ground, pondering the riddle. The sunlight slid from the woods. The shadows glided in. Still Half sat and thought, saying the raven's riddle over and over.

He was reciting it once again when who should appear but his two brothers. They had stumbled upon each other in the forest, and both were pretending they had not lost their way.

"Now here's one who'd make a fine master blacksmith. A lumpkin who sits on the ground muttering to himself," the eldest brother said.

"I'm trying to solve the riddle the raven told me," said Half.

"Oh, so now it's ravens that talk to you, is it?" said the second brother. "And just what did this raven have to say?"

"She told me about the Golden Heart of Winter that lies under the ground, beating so that spring will always come."

"Now there's a pretty tale," mocked the eldest brother. "Talking ravens and golden hearts."

"You are more of a half-wit than I thought," scoffed the second brother.

"But the tale is true. The raven is the heart's guardian. She was imprisoned in this very tree because she would not tell Death where the heart lies."

Half's two brothers jeered at him again, but each silently recalled the raven in the tree. And each in his own heart began to think the same thing: Could this fool's story be true? Could there really be a heart of gold that made the seasons turn? If so, it would be the most valuable thing in the world. And if I could find it, my father would certainly name me master of the forge.

"And did this raven tell you just where this golden heart lies?" asked the eldest brother craftily.

"Yes, did she?" echoed the second brother.

"No," answered Half. "But she gave me a riddle to solve."

"And what is the riddle?"

Without any hesitation, Half told them.

" 'Up and down / Left and right / They criss and cross / Both day and night,' " repeated the eldest brother.

" 'Under the sky / Under the ground / Under the starstone / It is found,' " finished the second brother.

"Yes, that's it. But I don't know what it . . ." Half did not finish his words, because suddenly both his brothers gave a great cry and tore through the dark wood. They did not stop until they reached the crossroads and the great rock that glittered like the night sky.

"The starstone!" cried the second brother.

The boulder was heavy, but their greed gave them strength, and the brothers swore and strained until they moved it aside. Then, with sword and dagger, they chopped and dug until at last they saw a gleam of gold, brighter than the rising moon.

"There, there! The Golden Heart!" shouted the eldest brother, shielding his eyes from the light.

The second scrabbled with his fingers until he brought up in his hand the heart, soft and warm and shining brighter than the sun. He could not look at it, but held it aloft and bellowed, "Mine! The Golden Heart is mine!"

Then his brother struck him.

They fell upon each other with sword and dagger until the second brother sank bleeding to the ground.

Clutching the Golden Heart, the eldest brother staggered to his feet. "Now you belong to me, and I shall be master," he gasped, and started to reel home.

He had taken but three steps when the Golden Heart began to flicker and dim and grow cold until it was like a lump of ice in his hand. It burned him to the bone. He shrieked and flung it down.

Then the moon sank, and a cold wind rose.

The eldest brother reached for his lantern and found it covered with ice. The wind threw him against the starstone, and the ice began to cover him as he clung to it.

In the forest Half felt the wind. "What is happening? Where have my brothers gone?" he cried.

"What have you done?" shrieked the raven, appearing at his side.

Before Half could say anything at all, the darkness thickened about him. A pale light began to rise and shape itself. At first it was a gray and whirling blur. But as it blew nearer, Half could see that it was Death on an ashen horse.

"Death, why do you ride?" Half cried.

"Because the Golden Heart is taken," Death answered.

"How?"

"By your brothers."

"Oh, no!"

"Now I will reign forever," said Death, and swirled off into the dark.

"The heart! The heart!" screamed the raven, streaking away through the trees.

His own heart fit to break, Half ran after her.

The road beyond the wood glowed with a strange chill light, and Half soon saw from what it came. Ice. Ice that sheathed the trees and pressed down the grass. Ice that stilled the birds in their nests, that froze the cattle in the fields. Half slipped often on the ice. He was bruised and sore, his clothes in tatters, his boots in shreds, but still he followed the shrieking raven.

He saw his eldest brother covered with ice and clinging to the starstone. He saw his second brother shrouded in ice upon the ground. He fell again, and his hand closed around something hard and cold.

"The heart!" croaked the raven, alighting on his shoulder and digging in with her claws.

Half held the heart to his ear and heard nothing. The heart was as silent as a grave. But the raven, cocking her head against it, rasped, "There is still time—if the heart can be thawed."

"My father!" Half shouted. "He is the master blacksmith of this land. He can do it!"

"Hurry, then," said the raven. "Think on spring so you, too, do not freeze on the way home."

Half obeyed. Racing home, he closed his mind to the cold. He saw instead the sun dappling the forest and bloodroot poking through the spring grass. At last he reached his house and stumbled into the forge. There, to his horror, he saw that the fire was out. The horses stood frozen in their stalls, and over the anvil his father lay, wearing a coat of ice. Weeping, he sank to his knees.

"Get up!" the raven commanded. "It is you who must take your father's place. You must warm the heart."

Half blinked at her. He had never been allowed to work at the forge.

"Hurry!" urged the raven.

Half rose. "I will try," he said. He had watched his father and brothers often enough so he knew at least where to begin. Grateful that the ice had not touched the hearth, he cleaned out the ashes as he had done many times before. Then he laid in wood shavings, sticks of oak and pine. He reached for the flint and steel to light the fire and found them frozen in place. He pried and scraped at them until his fingers were raw and bleeding. But at last he broke them free. Then, bending over the hearth, he struck the steel against the flint. Bright sparks fell into the kindling.

"Burn, burn," he whispered, and the wood began to flame. He fanned the fire with the bellows until it blazed. The heat began to melt the ice in the forge. Half laid the heart in the flames and waited. Then, face burnt, eyes tearing, he pulled it out. It was golden once more. But it was also still as stone.

"Beat, beat," he begged it.

But no sound came from the heart.

"Beat!"

The heart lay silent.

Turning his face upward, Half cried out, "Death, please. Take my own heart, but let spring come again."

And suddenly he heard, distant as a footfall in the next room, a tiny beat. Then another. And another. Louder they grew, and more forceful. The Golden Heart was alive once more!

"It lives because of your own golden heart," the raven whispered in his ear.

Then both raven and heart were gone.

The sun began to rise, and all things to return to life.

"Father," Half said quietly, greeting him as he rose from the anvil.

The blacksmith looked with wonder at his youngest son, now so tall and strong before him. Then he embraced him, and the two wept in each other's arms.

Soon the two elder sons came home, heads bowed, and begged their brother's forgiveness.

"I forgive you gladly," Half said, "if you forgive yourselves." His voice was firm and sure.

His brothers nodded, promising to make amends for all past deeds, and the three embraced and wept together as one.

And somewhere in the magical wood, the raven kept watch
over the newly buried Golden Heart while the leaves sprang green
on the trees and the birds sang songs of joy.